Win a Tiara Club Perfect Princess Prize!

There are six tiaras hidden in *Christmas Wonderland*, and each one has a secret word in it in mirror writing. Find all six words and re-arrange them to make a special Perfect Princess sentence, then send it to us. Each month, we will put the correct entries in a draw and one lucky reader will receive a magical Perfect Princess Prize!

Send your Perfect Princess sentence, your name and your address on a postcard to :
THE TIARA CLUB COMPETITION,
Orchard Books, 338 Euston Road,
London, NW1 3BH

Australian readers should write to:
Hachette Children's Books,
Level 17/207 Kent Street, Sydney, NSW 2000.

Only one entry per child.
Final draw: 30 September 2007

The Tiara Club

By Vivian French

PRINCESS CHARLOTTE AND THE BIRTHDAY BALL	ISBN	1 84362 863 5
PRINCESS KATIE AND THE SILVER PONY	ISBN	1 84362 860 0
PRINCESS DAISY AND THE DAZZLING DRAGON	ISBN	1 84362 864 3
PRINCESS ALICE AND THE MAGICAL MIRROR	ISBN	1 84362 861 9
PRINCESS SOPHIA AND THE SPARKLING SURPRISE	ISBN	1 84362 862 7
PRINCESS EMILY AND THE BEAUTIFUL FAIRY	ISBN	1 84362 859 7

The Tiara Club at Silver Towers

PRINCESS CHARLOTTE AND THE ENCHANTED ROSE	ISBN	1 84616 195 9
PRINCESS KATIE AND THE DANCING BROOM	ISBN	1 84616 196 7
PRINCESS DAISY AND THE MAGICAL MERRY-GO-ROUND	ISBN	1 84616 197 5
PRINCESS ALICE AND THE CRYSTAL SLIPPER	ISBN	1 84616 198 3
PRINCESS SOPHIA AND THE PRINCE'S PARTY	ISBN	1 84616 199 1
PRINCESS EMILY AND THE WISHING STAR	ISBN	1 84616 200 9

All priced at £3.99.

The Tiara Club books are available from all good bookshops, or can be ordered direct from the publisher: Orchard Books, PO BOX 29, Douglas IM99 1BQ. Credit card orders please telephone 01624 836000 or fax 01624 837033 or visit our Internet site: www.wattspub.co.uk or e-mail: bookshop@enterprise.net for details.

To order please quote title, author, ISBN and your full name and address. Cheques and postal orders should be made payable to "Bookpost plc.© Postage and packing is FREE within the UK (overseas customers should add £2.00 per book).

Prices and availability are subject to change.

What happens next in

Ruby Mansions?

Meet the friends of the Rose Room princesses in:

Princess Chloe

and the **Primrose Petticoats**

Princess Jessica

and the **Best-Friend Bracelet**

Princess Georgia

and the **Shimmering Pearl**

Princess Olivia

and the **Velvet Cloak**

Princess Lauren

and the **Diamond Necklace**

Princess Amy

and the **Golden Coach**

Check out

The Tiara Club

website at:

www.tiaraclub.co.uk

You“ll find Perfect Princess games and fun things to do, as well as news on the Tiara Club and all your favourite princesses!

The Tiara Club

Christmas Wonderland

For Princess Angie,
with much love
xxx VF

www.tiaraclub.co.uk

First published by Orchard Books in 2006

ORCHARD BOOKS
338 Euston Road, London NW1 3BH
Orchard Books Australia
Hachette Children's Books
Level 17/207 Kent St, Sydney NSW 2000

A Paperback Original

A CIP catalogue record for this book is available
from the British Library.

ISBN-10: 1 84616 296 3
ISBN-13: 978 1 8461 6 296 1

3 5 7 9 10 8 6 4

Orchard Books is a division of Hachette Children's Books

The Tiara Club

Christmas Wonderland

By Vivian French

ORCHARD BOOKS

The Royal Palace Academy for the Preparation of Perfect Princesses

(Known to our students as "*The Princess Academy*")

OUR SCHOOL MOTTO:

A Perfect Princess always thinks of others before herself, and is kind, caring and truthful.

Silver Towers offers a complete education for Tiara Club princesses with emphasis on selected outings. The curriculum includes:

Fans and Curtseys

A visit to Witch Windlespin

(Royal herbalist, healer and maker of magic potions)

Problem Prime Ministers

A visit to the Museum of Royal Life

(Students will be well protected from the Poisoned Apple)

Our headteacher, Queen Samantha Joy, is present at all times, and students are well looked after by the school Fairy Godmother, Fairy Angora.

Our resident staff and visiting experts include:

LADY ALBINA MACSPLINTER
(School Secretary)

CROWN PRINCE DANDINO
(School Excursions)

QUEEN MOTHER MATILDA
(Etiquette, Posture and Poise)

FAIRY G
(Head Fairy Godmother)

We award tiara points to encourage our Tiara Club princesses towards the next level. All princesses who win enough points at Silver Towers will attend the Silver Ball, where they will be presented with their Silver Sashes.

Silver Sash Tiara Club princesses are invited to return to Ruby Mansions, our exclusive residence for Perfect Princesses, where they may continue their education at a higher level.

PLEASE NOTE:
Princesses are expected to arrive at the Academy with a *minimum* of:

TWENTY BALL GOWNS
(with all necessary hoops, petticoats, etc)

TWELVE DAY DRESSES

SEVEN GOWNS
suitable for garden parties, and other special day occasions

TWELVE TIARAS

DANCING SHOES
five pairs

VELVET SLIPPERS
three pairs

RIDING BOOTS
two pairs

Cloaks, muffs, stoles, gloves and other essential accessories as required

Hello - and don't you just LOVE winter? I do - all that gorgeous crunchy snow and sparkly frost, and skating on the frozen lake...it's SUCH fun!

I'm Princess Charlotte, by the way - and I know who you are! You're a Perfect Princess, and you're keeping me and my friends company at Silver Towers.

You do remember my friends, don't you? There's Katie (she adores animals!) and Daisy (she's so sweet) and Alice (she's got the loveliest smile) and Sophia (she's amazingly pretty) and Emily, who's the kindest person ever. And you!

Chapter One

Like I said, winter is SO fabulous...and our winter term at Silver Towers was REALLY special! It had been wonderfully cold for ages, but not that horrid damp cold that makes you feel miserable. No – it was the bright and frosty kind, and the sky always seemed to be blue.

The lake in front of the Princess Academy froze over, and we had SUCH amazing skating parties. Even the horrible twins, Diamonde and Gruella, learned to skate, although they did tell us over and over again how very un-princessy it was.

And then the weather changed.

The first bell of the morning went, and we opened our eyes expecting Silver Rose Room to be bright and sunny as usual – but it wasn't. It was grey and gloomy.

Daisy hopped out of bed and pattered over to the window.

"It's really cloudy," she reported, "and it's POURING with rain!"

Katie snuggled deeper under her bedclothes.

"It was going to be the ice dancing competition this afternoon," Emily reminded us. "What'll happen now?"

We looked at each other blankly.

"I suppose the rain might stop," Sophia said.

"No chance," Daisy said from the window. "It looks as if it's going to rain for ever."

"Oh, BOTHER." I threw my pillow at Katie, who didn't move. "We'll probably have some horrible boring lesson instead."

Sophia stretched. "If we don't get up soon we'll get into trouble for being late for breakfast."

Alice was already heading for the bathroom. "Come on, you lot," she said. "Last one down for breakfast has to sit with snooty

old Diamonde and Gruella!"

Of course that got us moving, even Katie, and we arrived in the dining hall at exactly the same time. Almost all the other princesses were already there, but luckily we found a table

where we could sit together.

Diamonde floated in a few seconds later, followed by Gruella. As they passed our table Diamonde stuck her nose in the air.

"You must be SO disappointed," she sneered. "No more showing off on the ice! SUCH a shame."

"Bet they thought they'd win the competition," Gruella agreed.

Sometimes I say things before I've really thought about whether I should say them or not. Do you ever do that? Words just seem to pop out of my mouth before I can stop them.

"We can beat you at ANY competition," I said.

And at that moment our headteacher, Queen Samantha Joy, came sailing into the dining hall, with our school fairy godmother, Fairy Angora, behind her – and the head fairy godmother, Fairy G, as well.

"WOW!" Charlotte whispered. "Something REALLY important must be going to happen!"

Chapter Two

Queen Samantha Joy gave us a huge smile. "Now, my dear princesses – I'm sure you're all disappointed that there can be no ice dancing competition this afternoon. I can, however, announce another competition instead...a very special one! As you know, we are holding a Winter Festival assembly at the end of term, and we would like YOU to provide the entertainment."

We looked at each other in amazement.

"Think of it as a talent show," Queen Samantha Joy said. "You may work in a pair, or in a group, and on the day you will present a dance, or a song, or even a little play – it's up to you. And not only will it be the entertainment for your parents and friends, but it will also be a competition, and the first prize is – a visit to Christmas Wonderland!"

We were absolutely speechless. EVERYONE knows about Christmas Wonderland – it's utterly FABULOUS! There's the best ice skating rink in the whole wide world, and snow slopes with the sweetest little toboggans, and sleigh rides with REAL reindeer.

And that's only a bit of it! There are little wooden stalls selling hot chocolate with fluffy cream on top, and crunchy spicy gingerbread, and others selling heaps of toys and all kinds of pretty things.

Then there's a Christmas Fair with a big wheel covered in twinkling lights, and a carousel with the most BEAUTIFUL golden horses, and coconut shies and candyfloss stalls. And the best thing about it is that when you get there you're given a bag of silver tokens, and you pay for all the rides and presents and everything else you want with those. It's SO amazing!

Of course we all began talking at once. Our headteacher let us chat, but after five minutes or so Fairy G banged on a table with a spoon.

"Silence!" she boomed. (Fairy G has the loudest voice ever!) "Now, here are the rules. Are you listening?"

It was so quiet you could have heard a pin drop.

"Rule number one. Each group will perform for not less than five minutes, and not more than ten."

"Rule number two. Your performance must be all your own work. If you want to recite a poem, then YOU must write the poem. If you want to sing a song, you write the words and the music. If it's a play – you are the playwrights!

"Rule number three. You will also design any costumes or scenery you may need – but of course Fairy Angora and I will be here to help in any way we can." Fairy G stopped, and her beaming smile reached every corner of the dining hall. "And if you SHOULD need a tiny sprinkle or two of magic, I'm sure that can be arranged! Any questions?"

Diamonde had her hand up before anyone else. "Excuse me,"

she began, "but might I point out that a Perfect Princess is NOT expected to be an entertainer? At home Mummy has a master of ceremonies for what she calls High Jinks and Nonsense. She says HER role is to be a Gracious Presence."

Honestly – sometimes Diamonde is SO rude! We held our breath, and waited for Fairy G to explode, or for Queen Samantha Joy to be FURIOUS.

It was almost disappointing. Queen Samantha Joy just raised her eyebrows.

"So do I understand that you don't wish to take part in the competition, Princess Diamonde?" she said.

Diamonde went pink. You could tell she hadn't expected that sort of answer at all.

"Erm..." she began, and I could see her thinking about that

WONDERFUL prize! "Erm...well, I suppose I might...that is... perhaps it would be all right for me and Gruella to take part just this once."

"Excellent," Queen Samantha Joy said briskly. "It would have been MOST disappointing to find that one of my princesses did not feel able to share in a festive celebration."

Fairy G held up her wand. "Fairy Angora and I will be in the lower hall all afternoon," she said, "so if any of you need any help please come and find us there."

Fairy Angora nodded. "That's right, my little darlings. And I'll have some lovely LOVELY material for your costumes!"

As our headteacher and the two

fairy godmothers left the dining hall Diamonde and Gruella came stamping over to our table, and Diamonde hissed right in my face, "Remember what you said about beating us in any competition,

Princess Boastful Charlotte? Well, watch us win THIS competition and leave you for DEAD!"

"So THERE!" Gruella said, and the two of them flounced away.

Chapter Three

"Goodness me!" Sophia said, and she looked really shocked. "That's a dreadful thing to say!"

Alice folded her arms. "There's only one way to deal with Diamonde and Gruella," she said. "We've got to win this competition fair and square!"

"Quite right." Katie's lovely

green eyes were sparkling.

Daisy nodded, but Emily was looking thoughtful.

"Do we actually need to win?" she asked. "Wouldn't it be OK if we just beat Diamonde and Gruella?"

"I think we go for winning," Katie said firmly. "What do you think, Charlotte?"

I thought of the way Diamonde had glared at me. "Yes," I said. "Absolutely. And if we did win, we'd get to go to Christmas Wonderland too – wouldn't that be just so FABULOUS? All of us together?"

"It would be utter BLISS," Sophia sighed.

"Do you know what? I think THAT'S why we should try to win," Emily said in her quiet little voice. She went pink as we all looked at her. "Sorry...I just thought Perfect Princesses shouldn't worry about trying to teach stupid people like Diamonde a lesson. She's not worth bothering about."

There was a moment's silence, then Sophia gave Emily a HUGE hug. "You're completely and utterly right," she said, "and it only goes to prove you're the most Perfect Princess ever!"

I kept thinking about what Emily had said all the rest of the morning, and I couldn't help feeling just a little bit dreadful. It was I who had told Diamonde that we could beat her in any competition – so in a way I'd started it all, and that made me think I was SO not a Perfect Princess. I decided I was going to try really hard to Think of Others Before Myself.

By the time we met at lunchtime we were fizzing with ideas, and so was everybody else. Princess Freya actually pirouetted all the way down the corridor, and

Princess Jemima, Princess Sunita and Princess Lisa were so deep in a discussion about their play they let their soup go cold. Princess Nancy kept singing "Tra la lala!", and Princess Eglantine was scribbling furiously on a piece of paper.

"So," Katie said as we sat down together. "What are we going to do?"

"What about some kind of dance?" Daisy suggested. "Sophia's absolutely BRILLIANT at dancing!"

"Or a poem?" Sophia looked at me. "You're good at rhymes, Charlotte."

"If Charlotte wrote a poem, Daisy could make up a tune for it and turn it into a song," Emily said.

"And then we could dance while we sang it!" Alice's cheeks were glowing with excitement.

I gulped. "I'm not sure..."

"That'd be STUNNING!" Katie clapped her hands. "YOU write the poem, Charlotte, and Daisy can write the music, and then Sophia can work out a dance routine! And Alice can design the costumes, and Emily and I will help her and we'll make some kind of background as well!"

"YES!" Alice's eyes were like stars, and everyone else was

looking SO enthusiastic I didn't like to say anything. And it did sound fun – IF I could write some kind of poem!

"Why don't we all write the poem?" I said hopefully. "It's bound to be quicker that way.'

"Let's start NOW!" Alice jumped up. "Let's go and work in the recreation room."

And we trooped off to create the best poem ever.

It wasn't that easy. We chewed the ends of our pencils for AGES, but no ideas came. It didn't help that Diamonde and Gruella had followed us, and were sitting on the other sofa whispering.

"What about something about princesses?" I said at last.

"But what rhymes with princesses?" Daisy asked.

Alice sat up straight. "Dresses, of course!"

I began to scribble in my notebook.

"We are da di da princesses
See us in our Something dresses—"

"That sounds OK," Emily said encouragingly.

Sophia looked over my shoulder.

"What about, 'Silver Towers princesses?'"

"See us in our party dresses?" Daisy wondered.

"I know!" Katie grabbed the pencil out of my hand. "What about WINTER dresses? And we can put in something about snow, and skating, and holly—"

I snatched the pencil back. "So it's a poem all about winter, and Christmas, and it could end up wishing the audience a Very Merry Christmas and a Happy New Year!"

We sat back, feeling SO

proud of ourselves. I don't think any of us noticed how very quiet Diamonde and Gruella had suddenly become.

Chapter Four

After that it was non-stop work, but in the nicest way. I wrote out our poem, and Daisy made up the sweetest tune – it was so catchy it really did make you want to dance! Sophia spent ages working out our moves, and Alice covered huge sheets of paper with designs for the most WONDERFUL costumes.

Sophia, Emily and Katie were to have gorgeous white satin dresses with sparkly snowflakes scattered all over the skirts, and loads of fluffy net petticoats. Alice, Daisy and I would be dressed in fabulous dark green velvet with holly berry red silk sashes, and our petticoats would be layers and layers of bright red silk.

"And all the dresses will have hoop petticoats as well", Alice told us, "so when we twirl they'll look completely spectacular! Oh, and I want to stitch little twinkly crystals onto the green velvet, like dewdrops..." A dreamy look came over her face, and she began to make more notes on her drawings.

"Ooooh! DO look, Gruella! The horrible Silver Rose Roomers are going to have SPOTTY dresses!"

It was Diamonde, and she was staring at Alice's lovely drawings. I could see Alice wanted to hide them so Diamonde couldn't look, but she was too polite.

Gruella pushed Daisy out of the way. "What are THOSE things?" she asked.

"Snowflakes," Alice said. "And, now, if you'll excuse me, I'm going to choose my material."

"We'd HATE to get in your way," Diamonde sneered. "Of course, we've got OUR dresses planned already!"

I wasn't quite sure if she was telling the truth, because a moment later, as we were walking down to the lower hall, I saw Gruella pull a notebook out of her pocket and start drawing madly. For a moment I wondered if she was copying Alice's ideas, but I pushed the idea out of my head. Surely not even the twins would be as horrible as that!

We woke up on the day of the Winter Festival feeling SO excited!

We fairly bounced out of bed, and Sophia made us have one last rehearsal in our dormitory before we went down to breakfast.

> "We are Silver Towers princesses (*twirl, kick, twirl*),
> See us in our winter dresses (*kick, clap, kick*),

We are here to wish you well
(*slow curtsey*),
We've a winter tale to tell..."
(*hold out our arms to the audience*)

It went like clockwork from beginning to end, and as we finished with,

"So our wish is very clear,
A very merry Christmas,
and a Happy New Year!"

and sank into our final curtsies we couldn't help feeling just a teeny bit pleased with ourselves.

Our costumes were hanging up by our beds, and they were the most GORGEOUS dresses ever. Fairy G and Fairy Angora had both helped, and the snowflakes sparkled

and the dewdrops twinkled beautifully. Katie and Emily had made a row of the sweetest little Christmas trees as a background...oh, surely we HAD to win!

The Winter Festival was going to be held in the grand ballroom, and as we hurried along the corridor in our costumes we could hear the hum and rustle of the audience. I knew my parents were somewhere in there,

together with all the other kings and queens and princes and princesses, and I suddenly felt nervous.

When we got to the foyer, Fairy G was standing there holding a big clipboard.

"First on will be Silver Lupin Room," she boomed. "Then Lavender, then Poppy – except for Diamonde and Gruella; they'll be next – and finally Silver Rose Room." She looked round.

"Are Diamonde and Gruella here?"

"Yes, Fairy G," Diamonde and Gruella chorused. They were at the back of the foyer, wearing huge black cloaks.

"What are they going to do?" Katie whispered in my ear.

I shook my head. I hadn't seen either of them much for a couple of days. I knew they'd had their dresses specially made, because a MASSIVE parcel had arrived the day before, and they'd scuttled off with it to their dormitory. NOBODY had been allowed to see! Sophia had said she thought that was cheating, but apparently it was OK because they'd designed the costumes themselves.

Chapter Five

"Right! The rest of you tiptoe into the back of the ballroom," Fairy G instructed us. "You can watch until it's your turn. Now, who's first? Oh yes – Silver Lupin Room. That's you, Jemima, isn't it? Make sure you and Lisa and Sunita and the others are ready. Good luck to you all!"

We nodded, and hurried away to watch the others.

Silver Lupin Room's play was fun, although Lisa kept tripping over her long skirts. In fact, we would have enjoyed all the different performances if we hadn't been so nervous. We could see Queen Samantha Joy making notes, and whispering to a very important looking king sitting beside her, so we guessed they must be the judges.

At last there was only one group to go before us.

"Here we go!" Alice whispered in my ear.

I could hardly speak, I was so anxious. The lights dimmed, and music started to play. The crimson red curtains swept apart, and there were Diamonde and Gruella...

And one of them was dressed all in white satin, with snowflakes on her hooped skirts...and the other was in green velvet with a holly berry red silk sash!

They curtsied to the audience, who were applauding madly, and Gruella began to chant,

"We are Silver Towers princesses
See us in our winter dresses!"

Diamonde went on,

"We are here with a very clever story to tell

And we hope you will think we are doing it very well!"

It was AWFUL! It was almost EXACTLY what we'd planned, except we had a better tune, and they didn't dance – they just marched up and down. But it was EVERYTHING we'd thought of. I felt completely sick. How could

we go on now? Everyone would laugh! There was a massive lump at the back of my throat, and I was SO close to bursting into tears.

And then Diamonde stopped! Honestly. After just two lines.

She stopped dead, and looked like a rabbit that had seen the fiercest wolf in the whole wide world. She had SO obviously forgotten her words. The audience began to shift in their seats, and Diamonde looked more and more desperate...and I knew she must be wanting the floor to swallow her up.

And that's when I knew what I had to do.

I stood up in the back of the grand ballroom, and I sang in my loudest voice,

"We are Silver Towers
princesses
See us in our winter dresses!"

And I twirled and kicked my legs as I danced up the middle of the central aisle in the grand ballroom.

I knew my friends were following because I could hear them singing with me...

> "We are here to wish you well—"

we sang, and as we reached the front of the stage, we curtsied to Diamonde and Gruella.

"We've a winter tale to tell..."

We climbed up the steps, and as we held out our hands to the audience the twins unfroze, and copied us.

On we sang, and we danced like we'd never danced before, and we spun Diamonde and Gruella round so it really truly looked as if they knew what they were doing.

At the end, as we sang,

"So our wish is very clear
A very merry Christmas,
And a Happy New Year!"

we sank into the DEEPEST curtsies, and Diamonde and Gruella curtsied with us.

The applause was amazing!

Everybody there clapped and cheered, and we curtsied and CURTSIED until at last the curtain fell. And as it fell, the weirdest thing happened.

Gruella went BRIGHT red, and stamped her foot, and shouted at Diamonde.

"I TOLD you we shouldn't copy what they did! I KNEW you'd forget the words!"

For a moment none of us knew what to do. I could see Fairy G and Fairy Angora, and Fairy Angora was looking HORRIFIED. Fairy G wasn't, though. She didn't look at all surprised.

And then Diamonde squealed, and rushed off the stage, and Gruella dashed after her.

When it came to the grand finale, and we were asked to come onto the stage for the results of the competition, neither of the twins was there.

Chapter Six

There was a burst of trumpets, and Queen Samantha Joy stood up. "My dear princesses," she began, and she sounded very pleased and proud. "You have EXCELLED yourselves, and I wish it were possible for every single one of you to go to Christmas Wonderland.

Unfortunately, the prize is for one group only...and it gives me SUCH pleasure to announce the winner."

She paused, and we held our breath, although I KNEW we weren't going to win. How could we? Our presentation had got all muddled up with Diamonde and Gruella's.

"We have chosen the winners for a very special reason," our headteacher went on. "Here at Silver Towers, we believe the most important lesson we can teach is that Perfect Princesses should always think of others before themselves. Tonight there has been a wonderful demonstration of just such thought. We award the first prize to...SILVER ROSE ROOM!"

For a moment we stood completely still. Then we screamed. I know – Perfect Princesses do NOT scream, but we did. I'm very sorry, but we just couldn't help it. And then we hugged each other and curtsied to

Queen Samantha Joy and waved madly to our parents and grandparents. The audience went wild. They clapped and clapped and CLAPPED, and we curtsied over and over again and did more hugging...it was MAGIC!

*

That night, as we lay tucked up in bed in Silver Rose Room, Alice asked, "Does anyone know what happened to Diamonde and Gruella?"

"Freya's mum told my mum they've been sent home," Sophia said sleepily. "She said Gruella admitted to Fairy G that she'd copied Alice's pictures, and after that Diamonde confessed that she'd cheated."

"Oh well," Katie said. "It all turned out all right in the end."

"Thanks to Charlotte," Emily said, and blew me a kiss.

"The Perfect Princess," Daisy added.

And as I sank into sleep, I knew that no dream could EVER be as wonderful as my real life.

Five wonderful friends, and you...and we're ALL going to Christmas Wonderland!

Hello - and isn't it just SO exciting? We're going to Christmas Wonderland! Hurrah hurrah and DOUBLE hurrah! And it's BRILLIANT that you're coming too. It wouldn't be the same without you.

I'm Princess Alice. Did you guess? And you've met Charlotte, Katie, Daisy, Emily and Sophia - so all we have to do now is ENJOY OURSELVES! I mean, what could possibly go wrong when we're all on holiday together?

Chapter One

When we won the trip to Christmas Wonderland, at first we couldn't believe it. Even when we were in the coach and on the way, it didn't seem real. It was only as we swept through the sparkly gates that we suddenly realised – here we were!

It was SO extraordinary!

Outside the gates it was an ordinary sort of drizzly day, but inside the sky was blue, and the sun was shining – and the ground was covered in SNOW! Snow as white as the very best sort of icing sugar.

We all began to talk at once and tell each other what we could see out of the windows. Fairy G and Fairy Angora, who'd come along to look after us, laughed.

"Isn't it lovely?" Fairy G beamed. "And are you looking forward to staying in an Ice Palace, my dears?"

We were TOTALLY silent.

"An ICE palace?" Charlotte said at last, her eyes wide.

"That's right," Fairy G said. "Look – you can just see the towers!"

We absolutely FLEW to the side of the coach, and there were these magical ice towers soaring into the clear blue sky. They were so sparkly we couldn't look at them for long – they were truly DAZZLING!

"Isn't it really cold inside?" Emily asked.

Fairy Angora shook her head. "I don't know how they do it, but it's wonderfully warm and cosy. The bedrooms all have white furry rugs, and glowing lanterns – you'll LOVE them, my little darlings.

A thought popped into my head. "Will we be in a dormitory? Like at school?"

"Oh, I DO hope so," Katie said. "It won't be half so much fun if we're in separate rooms."

Fairy G and Fairy Angora looked at each other, and I knew something wasn't quite right.

Fairy G said, "The dormitories sleep five to a room, not six, so we'll have to put one of you in a single room next door."

"Oh!" Katie sounded shocked. "But how will we choose who has the single room?"

Fairy Angora smiled her lovely smile. "I've thought it all out,"

she said, and she fished a heap of folded pieces of paper out of her bag. "One of these has a little bed drawn on it – and the person who chooses that one has the single room!" She piled the papers onto the seat of the coach, and we each took one...and guess what?

I had the picture of the little bed. "It's me," I said, and I suddenly felt as if I was going to cry.

Is that babyish? It probably is, and not at all what a Perfect Princess should do. Only I know what fun we have when we're all together, and I SO didn't want to be left out.

"You can be in our room right until we have to go to sleep," Charlotte promised.

"We'll miss you terribly!" Daisy said, and Katie and Emily nodded in agreement.

"Of course we will, but you'll

only be next door, and we can leave our doors open." Sophia gave my arm a comforting little squeeze.

I began to feel better, and just at that moment we passed a sleigh full of happy looking people – and the sleigh was pulled by six reindeer, with red velvet harnesses covered in tinkling

bells! It looked SUCH fun I forgot about being on my own.

"What shall we do first?" Fairy G asked. "Would you like to take a sleigh ride so we can see where everything is?"

"Oh yes, PLEASE!" we chorused, and the coach stopped. We were in front of the Ice Palace, and it looked FABULOUS! We tumbled out, and hurried through the glittering front door. A tall footman dressed in red and green bowed to us as we arrived in the hallway.

"You must be the Silver Towers princesses," he said. "Welcome to the Ice Palace at Christmas Wonderland! Please follow me to your rooms."

Chapter Two

Fairy Angora was right. The palace was wonderfully warm, and it was SO beautiful. There were thick rugs scattered over the polished wooden floors, and ruby lanterns glowed from every shelf. You could only really tell it was made of ice when you looked up to the ceiling, and saw these amazing frills and rosettes and whirls and twirls – all carved out of ice!

When we got upstairs it was just as lovely. The footman showed Fairy G and Fairy Angora to their

rooms, and they both had the most luxurious looking beds heaped with velvet cushions.

"Fairy Angora and I will get ready," Fairy G announced, "and then we'll set off."

The dormitory was the next door along the corridor – there were SO many doors! – and that was gorgeous too. All the beds were four-posters, with the prettiest pink silk and satin

patchwork covers, and in the corner was a huge squashy sofa piled high with cushions. The windows looked out to the snow slopes, and we rushed to see.

There were loads of toboggans absolutely whizzing down – and then we saw the sweetest little snow-white ponies waiting patiently at the bottom to tow the toboggans back up again. We could hardly believe our eyes. It was SO perfect!

"PLEASE can we go tobogganing?" I begged. "It looks SUCH fun!"

"We're going to do EVERYTHING!" Katie said. "That's why we're here!"

The footman coughed politely. "Excuse me, Your Highness," he said, "but would you like to see your room?"

"Oh!" I said. I'd quite forgotten I wasn't going to be in the big room. "Yes. Thank you very much."

He picked up my case, and I followed him, and my room wasn't next door at all.

It was right at the other end of the corridor.

It was a very sweet room. If I'd been staying in the Ice Palace with my grandparents I'd have loved it, but it did feel SO different from the dormitory. It had a dear little bed with a draped sky-blue canopy – but I knew that when

I woke up in the morning I'd feel really lonely. The footman bowed, and left me, and I slowly began to put my things away, thinking about how Katie and Charlotte and the others would be chattering and laughing together.

Suddenly, I remembered something! The big comfy sofa!

I'd ask Fairy G if I could sleep there! Halfway out of the door I stopped. What if Fairy G was changing? On the top of the chest of drawers was some writing paper and a pencil. Before I could change my mind I took a sheet of paper, and wrote:

I folded the paper in half, and dashed back up the corridor. All the doors were shut, but I was sure I remembered which was Fairy G's room, and I slipped my letter under her door. It caught on something for a second, but then it was gone. I skipped back down the corridor, feeling SO much better. I was so certain Fairy G would say yes I didn't even put my pyjamas under my pillow.

"I won't tell the others yet," I told myself. "I'll let it be a surprise."

A couple of minutes later Fairy Angora knocked on my door. "Time to go, Princess Alice," she called. I grabbed my coat and muff, and hurried out.

Fairy G, Charlotte, Emily, Sophia and Katie were already sitting in the sleigh. I gave Fairy G a hopeful look, but she was busy arranging a fluffy rug over her knees and didn't notice.

I squashed in next to Charlotte, and sighed happily. "Isn't this the best?"

Charlotte grinned. "It would be if you didn't take up so much room!"

Fairy Angora looked almost as excited as we did. "Are we all here?" she asked. "Oh! Where's

Princess Daisy?"

"She was in the bathroom when we came downstairs," Emily said. "She said she'd follow us."

"Shall I go and look for her?" I suggested.

But just then Daisy appeared – and she looked as if she'd been crying.

Chapter Three

Of course we asked Daisy what was wrong, but she wouldn't say. Instead she blew her nose, and said she was fine.

The only empty seat was opposite me, but instead of sitting there Daisy gave me SUCH an odd look. It was almost as if she was angry with me. Then she went to the back of the sleigh, and squeezed in next to Emily. It was so unlike her I didn't know what to think.

"Off we go!" Fairy G said cheerfully, and the jolly looking driver shook the reins. The bells rang a little tune, and the reindeer began to trot along

the snow-covered road. We went in and out of the toboggan slopes, and we couldn't help laughing at the rosy-cheeked toddlers who were falling over and making snow angels. Then we went past the ice rink, and it was so wonderful it almost made me want to jump out of the sleigh

straightaway. If I'd had my skates I would have! Then we came to the Christmas Fair, and the very first thing we saw was the big wheel, and

it looked ENORMOUS!

"You can see the whole of Christmas Wonderland from the top," Fairy Angora told us, and Charlotte and I smiled at each other. We couldn't wait!

"Would anyone like a drink of hot chocolate?" Fairy G asked as we began to swish our way in between the little wooden stalls. "You could have a look round, as well, if you like." She bent down to dig in her huge basket,

and pulled out six sparkling silver bags.

"Here are your Wonderland tokens. You pay for anything you want with these. No money needed!"

I heaved another HUGE sigh of happiness. It was SO fantastic. And I knew just what I wanted to buy. I wanted to find the best Christmas presents ever for all my lovely friends.

The sleigh stopped, and we climbed out. Of course we had to pat the reindeer, and they lowered their heads so we could scratch them behind their big furry ears.

Their eyes were huge, and they almost seemed to be smiling at us.

"Hot chocolate!" Fairy G said firmly, and shooed us towards the nearest stall. I stopped to wait for Daisy and Emily, but Daisy hurried past me and went to talk

to Sophia. I was really surprised, and Emily looked puzzled.

"Is Daisy OK?" I asked. Emily rubbed her nose.

"I don't know," she said. "Something's upset her, but she won't say what."

"But we always tell each other EVERYTHING," I said.

Emily nodded. "I know." She hesitated, and blushed. "I think it might be something to do with you, Alice."

"ME?" I stared at Emily, and then I remembered how Daisy had looked at me when she got into the sleigh.

But what could I have done?

I felt TERRIBLE. We'd all been best friends for ages and AGES. I decided it must be some awful misunderstanding, and there was only one way to find out. I had to find Daisy, and ask her – but when I got to the chocolate stall she wasn't there.

"She's gone to do some secret Christmas shopping," Fairy G said when I asked her where Daisy was. She handed me a big mug of steaming hot

chocolate, covered with thick cream and chocolate sprinkles. "Sophia's gone as well, but in the other direction. We're meeting them back here in an hour."

"Actually, I'd love to do some secret shopping," I said. I could see some utterly GORGEOUS little bags hanging from a rail

outside a stall just a little way away, and I was dying to have a proper look. Also I thought I could look for Daisy, and maybe we could have a chat, and I could find out what was wrong.

"Can I go too?" Katie's eyes were sparkling. "I want to buy some VERY secret things!"

"And me!" Charlotte said, and Emily nodded.

"The sleigh'll be back here about three o'clock," Fairy G said. "DON'T BE LATE!"

"We won't," we promised, and I wandered away, sipping my chocolate as I went.

Chapter Four

It was SO hard to choose! The little bags were utterly blissful, but then I saw some gorgeous scarves...and then there were some pretty PRETTY necklaces and bracelets. It took me ages to make up my mind, but in the end I bought a silver charm bracelet for each of my friends. I found a particularly lovely one for Daisy; it had tiny silver and white enamel daisies, and it was SO sweet. I knew she'd love it.

I only just got back to the chocolate stall on time; Fairy G was already beginning to stamp about and look at her watch in

a very obvious kind of way.

"Sorry!" I panted as I stuffed my parcels into the sleigh.

"Hm'ph!" Fairy G said. "Well, you're not quite the last! Has anyone seen Princess Daisy?"

None of us had.

Fairy G made a tutting noise.

"We'll give her a few more minutes, " she said. "After all, we are on holiday."

But Daisy didn't come back.

After twenty minutes we were getting really worried. It wasn't like Daisy; she's usually on time for everything.

"Do you think the poor little darling could have got lost?" Fairy Angora asked.

Sophia shook her head. "None of us did," she pointed out. "It's REALLY easy to find your way – there are signposts everywhere."

"She was looking as if she'd been crying when she came out of the Ice Palace," Katie said thoughtfully. "As if something had upset her."

"But what could it be? " Fairy G asked. "She was bursting with excitement in the coach on the way here."

I swallowed hard. "Emily thinks it might be something I've done."

"YOU?" Everyone stared at me in surprise, and then turned to Emily.

Emily went very pink. "It was just that Daisy was reading a piece of paper in our dormitory," she said, "and I thought it looked like Alice's writing. Daisy stuffed it in her pocket when she saw me looking, and rushed into the bathroom."

Have you ever been accused of something, and you KNOW you haven't done anything wrong, but you still feel guilty? It was weird. I felt AWFUL. All my friends were looking at me, and so were

Fairy G and Fairy Angora. I could feel myself beginning to blush.

"The only thing I've written was my note to Fairy G," I said. "Truly!"

Fairy G raised her eyebrows. "A note to me, Princess Alice? "

I nodded. "Yes – asking if I could sleep on the sofa in the dormitory with all my friends."

"But I never got a note," Fairy G said. "Are you sure you're not making a mistake?"

Chapter Five

I felt hot and cold all at the same time, and my mind began to whizz in mad little circles. For a second I wondered if I could have written a horrid note to Daisy without knowing I'd done it, but I KNEW I hadn't.

I took a deep breath. "Please, Fairy G," I said, "I really did write you a note. I don't know what Daisy was reading, but it absolutely wasn't anything from me. Please, I think we need to find her, and then we can ask her what's going on."

Fairy G gave me one of her piercing stares, where you feel as if she's looking right into the back of your head. Then she nodded.

"Very sensibly said, Princess Alice. You're quite right. I'll stay here, and Fairy Angora will take the sleigh back to the Ice Palace in case Daisy's gone there. The five of you have a good look round, but please come back to check with me every fifteen minutes."

It was SO sad; none of us felt happy any longer – we were so anxious about poor Daisy. Charlotte took my arm as we hurried away.

"Don't worry," she said. "We all know you'd NEVER do anything to upset Daisy."

"That's right." Katie and Sophia and Emily were right behind me. "In half an hour we'll be sitting on top of the big wheel with Daisy and wondering what the fuss was all about!"

It was very kind of them, but it almost made me feel worse...and then I realised what Katie had said.

"The big wheel!" I beamed. "Katie – you're a GENIUS! Fairy Angora said you can see the whole of Christmas Wonderland from the top. We can see where Daisy is!"

We zoomed towards the wheel, and it felt like AGES before it eventually stopped and we could get on. We settled ourselves in our sky boat, and the wheel began to turn again.

"Katie and Charlotte, you look that way," I instructed. "Emily and Sophia, if you look the other side, I'll look straight ahead."

Up we went, up and up...and it was JUST like flying! We were so high my stomach began to fill with butterflies, and I was glad to see Sophia was gripping the rail almost as tightly as I was.

And then I saw Daisy. She was sitting all by herself behind the candyfloss stall, and she looked SO lonely.

"There she is!" I yelled.

Of course we had to wait for the wheel to stop before we could get off, and that seemed to take ages as well. We scrambled out and dashed for the candyfloss stall, and were JUST in time to see Daisy get up and walk slowly away.

"DAISY!" we shouted, "DAISY! Come back!"

Daisy turned round, and we could see she'd been crying again. Her poor nose was bright red, and she was clutching a soggy hankie in one hand.

In the other was a torn piece of scribbled on paper – AND I SAW IT WAS MY HANDWRITING!

Chapter Six

"Daisy! I puffed as I ran towards her. "Daisy – what's that piece of paper?"

For a moment I thought she was going to run away, but she didn't. She sniffed, and handed me the paper.

"I NEVER guessed you didn't like me, " she said, and began to sob.

I stared at the paper, and Charlotte and Katie looked over my shoulder while Sophia and Emily put their arms round Daisy and gave her a clean hankie.

"Oh, DAISY!" I said, and I didn't know if I should laugh or cry. "This is my note for Fairy G – I must have put it under the wrong door! And it's only

HALF of it! I was asking if I could sleep on the sofa in your room because I didn't want to be on my own and be left out..."

Daisy eyes grew wider and WIDER – and then she gave me the BIGGEST hug. We all began to

laugh, and as we hurried back to Fairy G we linked arms and went on laughing. It was SO brilliant; all of a sudden we were back to being the Tiara Club on holiday, and I'm absolutely certain the others felt as happy as I did.

Fairy G laughed too when we told her what had happened, and seconds after we'd arrived Fairy Angora came swooshing over the snow in the sleigh, waving a crumpled piece of paper.

"I found this caught under the dormitory door," she said, "and I was SURE it was a clue!"

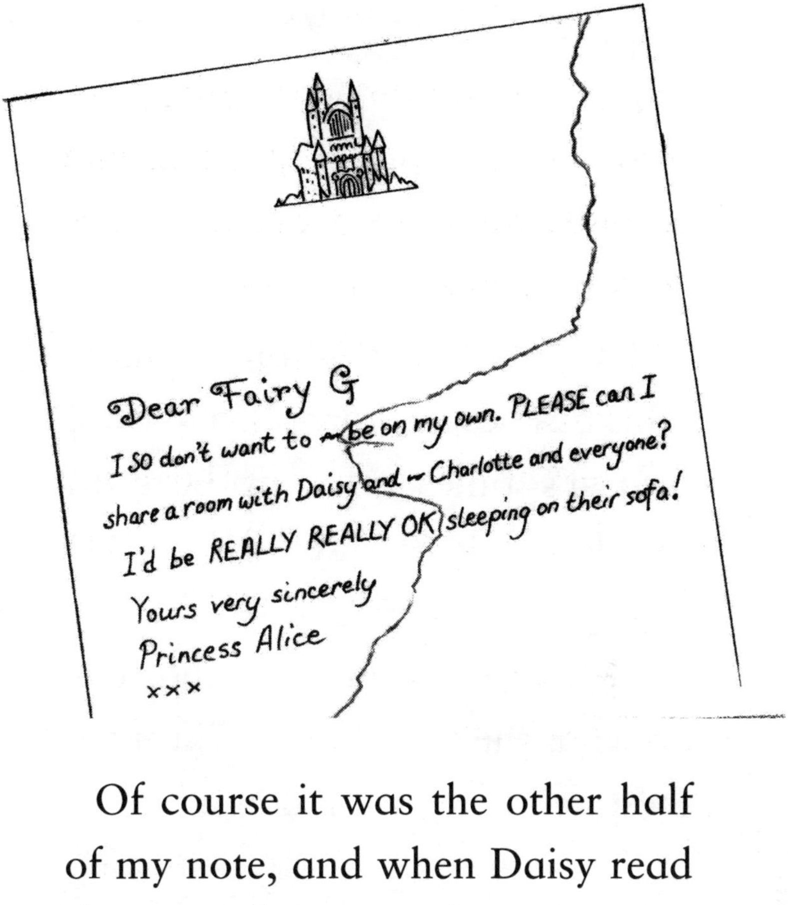

Of course it was the other half of my note, and when Daisy read the two bits together she just couldn't stop hugging me.

"I'm so SORRY, Alice," she kept saying.

And I kept saying I was sorry too, until Fairy G boomed, "ENOUGH!"

We were very quiet.

"It seems to me," Fairy G said, "this has been a storm in a teacup! And it's time we went back to the Ice Palace. HURRY INTO THE SLEIGH!"

When Fairy G talks like that you do what she says, but we did enjoy the ride home. We made all kinds of plans for the next day – starting with another ride on the big wheel!

And when we got back to the Ice Palace, guess what Fairy G did?

Yes! You're quite right.

She waved her wand, and the big squashy sofa in the dormitory suddenly turned into a neat little bed.

"SSSH!" she said, and put her finger to her lips. "Don't tell anyone! And remind me to change it back when we leave!"

We promised...and then we hurried to change into our very best evening gowns for the Ice Palace Welcome Ball.

Did we dance until midnight?

Of course we did!

And as the clock struck twelve we gave each other our presents, and Daisy just ADORED her bracelet.

"Tiara Club for ever!" Katie cheered.

"Yes," I agreed, "and BEST FRIENDS FOR EVER as well!"

And that means you too... and I do hope we see you again SOON!